things left unsaid

things left unsaid

sienna scanu

Published by Tablo

TABLE OF CONTENTS

[CHAPTER 1

sunshine and roses]

Leonardo, how could I explain my love for you, though you may not have treated me all that well, for some reason I had this compelling feeling that continued to grow inside of me, to love and to care for you to the best of my abilities. It was like an obligation. You sometimes doubted yourself which use to infuriate me because in my eyes you were perfect, and how could someone so perfect doubt themselves? I hope for the time we spent together; your feelings were somewhat real. I know mine were otherwise I wouldn't be here writing today. Even though we have no contact, and we no longer speak, my love for you is just as in control of my emotions as when your name used to appear on my screen, and occasionally your sweet comments about my appearance that gave me a reason to keep going are now gone. Now I feel lost, I wish I could say that I felt numb, but I didn't, the ache in my heart was as present as ever. I felt like there was no more reason to live, and my happiness was robbed from right under me and there was nothing I could do to fix it.

You were my happiness, my distraction, and my motivation in my tangled life and unfortunately when you walked out the door all the joy I had whilst being with you walked right out with you. Which is not your fault, how could you have known you had this much of an impact on just some girl's life. I really from the bottom of my heart hope I meant something to you, because to me you were the most beautiful boy. I think my heart may continue to ache over your absence which is something out of my control. But you have no idea how much I am in desperate need of your presence. You made life just that little bit better, and no matter how much I try no one's ability to attempt to put a smile on my face, beats the one that use to appear naturally while we would talk about the simplest things. I really did see a future with you and for the first time in my existence on this messed up planet I had hope Leonardo, I finally saw that light at the end of the tunnel that everyone talks about.

The thing I cherish and hold on to, is the fact that I got to see you in real life, and it was no longer through a phone which is usually how love stories go these days. To be completely honest I don't know if I would classify you as my first love, because first loves usually have some incredible stories or happy endings, but this ending just doesn't sit right with me. I don't think it ever will. The best way I could describe this feeling to you is that it's as if it was the first time my heart began beating for someone else other than me. It's like I was always living life in black and white and then I met you and suddenly I saw life in colour. But once I accepted the fact that we weren't going to talk ever again, things began to turn back to black and white. Leonardo words cannot express how much love I have in my heart to give to you, writing these words down on paper doesn't do it justice.

My only hope is that somewhere in your heart you feel some form of guilt or remorse but let me enhance one thing I don't wish bad upon anyone let alone you, I wish you find a girl that makes you happy or if you don't find someone, I urge you to continue with your dreams and aspirations and I hope they all come true. Even though you don't have me by your side to support you, I hope you find someone that loves you just as much as I do… or did. But honestly, I don't think you could ever find someone that loves you just as I did, someone that's in love with every inch of you, your fair hair, your big beautiful brown eyes with a hint of green in the middle, the brightest smile with the most perfect teeth but the best of it all was your personality. Your humour and your ability to make me laugh even on the worst day, that's what I loved about you. Truly I do wish that we could have just one last conversation, I just want to know where this love story all went wrong. From giving me all your attention, to you having all of mine to then just cutting me off, it had to have hurt right?

There is an infinite number of possibilities or excuses I've tried to make for you in my head but none of them sufficient enough to explain why I was cut off. But I don't know how you live your life every day without feeling like somethings missing. Or maybe you do, and I just don't know. But you no longer wake up to a good morning text on your phone, no more having someone constantly check up on you and someone to always be there to listen. I honestly don't know how you haven't taken up one of the numerous opportunities you have had to get into contact with me. I know apparently you don't want to talk to me because you don't want to "catch feelings" which it's too late for that now Leo.

But you know what, I think you didn't come back to me because you were guilty and you had no explanation to give me, so you simply thought if I cut her off and we don't talk, I won't have to make an excuse anymore. I don't know if you have ever heard of the famous phrase "sometimes things are best left unsaid" but in this situation I don't think that applies. I think you wouldn't have had the courage to cut things off with me if we had of had that one last conversation. I know when we first met, you had told me you weren't looking for anything serious and once I heard that a tear rolled down my face, I thought that was the worst outcome out of this whole situation. Little did I know what was waiting for me right around the corner. Leonardo left me 2 months after that conversation.

[CHAPTER 2

memories]

One of my favourite memories was when I hurt my knee and I told Leo about it, he was babying me, I forgot about the fact that I had a sore knee and I focused on him telling me everything was going to be okay. I don't know if you have ever heard of the placebo effect, where you give a false replacement treatment than the usual one, and in the patients mind they feel better even though, they haven't received any real treatment. He was like my placebo effect. He could tell me everything was going to get better in the worst situation, and I would believe him with my whole heart. Another one of my favourite memories was when I had a soccer match and I asked him for his advice, he was giving me all his tips and tricks. I knew damn well I wasn't going to use not a single one of them. But I just admired the fact that Leonardo took time out of his day to give me advice and that's what meant most to me. He said to me the 4 words that were just 4 words before they left Leonardo's lips. Once my game finished Leonardo said, "I'm proud of you" and that meant more to me than anyone else. His validation and his words meant more to me than anyone else's. When I had a science test the night before I was stressing out, and Leonardo knew exactly how to calm me down within the matter of words. So, the next day once I did my science test, all I could think about was when Leonardo said to me "everything's going to be okay, your smart, you know the answers, don't overthink it" And the second I got a 98 on that sheet of paper, I couldn't wait to get home to tell him. See it's the things like this, that make life just that little bit more enjoyable.

I remember him trying to always get me back, one weekend I had an event and I sent Leonardo a photo with a pretend wine glass in my hand, and he strongly advised me not to drink. And of course, I wasn't going to, but for the fun of it I lead him to believe I was, he wasn't too happy about it. The weekend after I attended my event, Leonardo attended a little party of his own, and of course being the little spiteful person, he was. He sent me a photo with a beer in his hand and immediately I broke out laughing because I knew he absolutely despised beer. Even though we are the way we are now, I don't think I would ever want to change, and go back and re-do that event I attended because I don't think I would have enjoyed it as much as when I was talking to Leonardo. Okay I think for the sake of both me and you, whoever's reading this let's shorten his name to Leo.

Sometimes I honestly think to myself, maybe Leo and I were better off as friends or possibly even strangers. But reminiscing these memories, even though we didn't have an enjoyable ending, well at least I know I didn't. It may not have been a long time but for me it was a good one. I knew it wouldn't last forever, but I hoped we had longer.

These memories will forever be stored inside my mind. I could never forget them even if I tried. Like the night before Leo and I met for the first time I went and bought a completely new outfit. And I rushed home tried it on and showed him. Everyone has someone that they care about their validation, for me Leo was my someone. Who's yours?

[CHAPTER 3

reality]

Now I've made this whole story out to be sunshine and roses, which it was for the beginning and maybe into the middle. But remember earlier in the story I said everything turned from black and white to colour and then when it was over everything went back to black and white.

Well, this chapter will show you just how I felt as it was beginning to transition to black and white.

Leos probably thinking in his head, I mean I wouldn't want to speak on your behalf Leo, I know you hate when people do that, but this is what I imagine you would say. Woah she's crazy we only met once; we weren't as close as she made out to be. I'm telling you Leo, you and only you when I say you meant everything to me, I genuinely mean it. But there was only so long I could keep making excuses for you. Everyone kept telling me that I should hate you, and I should never even attempt to contact you again after what you did to me. That what you did was extremely unfair to me, I'm sure you whoever's reading this by the end of this chapter would agree. Technically that was all true, but I could never bring myself to hate you. I wasn't angry I was just disappointed. I'm disappointed that Leo never explained anything, he saw me that day we met and then I was blocked.

Let me get back to explaining the day we met, or the times I had attempted to see Leo and these crazy excuses came in between it. So, I had endeavoured to see him the first 4 times I planned, one of the times he got as close to me as outside the shopping complex. But then apparently for some odd reason Leo had to hop on the next bus. So, I guess you could say I got stood up 1 out of the 4 times. The other 3 I got cancelled on the day before or the same morning. So yes, I painted a picture that he was the most perfect boy, but it's like painting with oil on a water canvas, no matter how hard you try it's never going to work. The morning of the day I got to see Leo, he tried cancelling on me, with the worst excuse imaginable. As you can imagine I was done just putting my head down and accepting whatever he told me, because I was in love with this perfect version of him, I made in my head. I had to talk to him with some sense of reality to it all, and reality hit me when I realised, I can't keep making plans to see Leo if he's never going to show up. It's mentally draining, and I wasn't prepared to put myself through that. Leo finally decided to come. I had no idea he was going to come in company of 6 other guys, that would have been my last expectation.

Now Leo you can deny a lot of things, you can deny you ever liked me, you can deny that we were never together. But one thing you cannot deny is the way you looked at me when you first saw me, I texted you and said "look up I see you" you raised your eyes and they met mine and suddenly a smile appeared on your face, and you began walking over to me.

You rubbed your hands against the side of your pants as if your palms were sweating, and you looked a bit pale. For a second there I thought you might pass out on me. I was just as nervous as you were, but I think I was just a bit better at hiding it. Now as much as I've talked down on you Leonardo in this past chapter, one thing I myself can't deny is how I fell extremely hard the second I saw you. You were perfect, your features were just as beautiful as they were through a phone. You were tall, tall enough that my neck ached from looking up at you. Sure, maybe I was a little mad that he brought all his friends to see me, but at that moment I didn't care. Now back to us meeting, I walked up to him and wrapped my arms around him. In my head I thought this hug was going to be quite short. But Leo you held on surprisingly a little longer, and a little tighter than I did.

Leo then continued to ask me how I was doing, and what I had gotten up to prior to seeing him. I was so nervous I had never stuttered in my life, but in that moment all I could manage to get out was "I'm good... uh thank you" Although I had just blurted out 4 words, if you count the "uh" it still didn't feel not one bit awkward.

They say you get this feeling inside of you when you meet the person you love. If you had showed up maybe the first or the second time. I guarantee you Leonardo I would have had that feeling. But unfortunately, all I had was this sick feeling in my stomach, as if it wasn't meant to be.

So, after that hug, that lasted long enough for me to hear his heart racing. And we had that little conversation. After three months of waiting thinking something magical was going to happen. I'm sorry to disappoint everyone when i say this but he walked away. he didn't answer not a single one of my messages. As you could imagine I was confused. Deeply confused. I kept asking myself, was it because of how I looked? Did I say something wrong? Am I not good enough for him? A lot of questions but no answers.

Later that night he sent me 2 blank photos, no responses to my hundreds of messages. I decided to back off and let Leo cool for the night and try again the next day.

So, the next day I was seeking to get a reply. And instead of a reply I got blocked. With no absolute explanation. Just a pending sign right next to his name. what would you do, if you were me?

[CHAPTER 4

mourning and wishes]

Now even though Leo walked out on me for the first time we met after 3 months, you're probably thinking, she was mad right? I wasn't, I really wasn't. I was dwelling on the fact that, okay he walked out on me, but I met him right. That must count for something. There was nothing anyone could say to make me hate him. Even though I was blocked I still tried to contact him. I even tried to get one of his owns friends to talk to him. But nothing would budge him. The thing that annoys me the most about this whole thing is that I don't have one ounce on anger in me.

Now normally after a girl, or a guy gets their heart broken. The first idea is to find yourself a rebound, I wish I could say that worked at the start, and "distracted me" but sooner or later I had to accept the fact that he left me, and there was absolutely nothing I could do about it. I'm glad that I didn't cave and follow the path of what almost everyone else does in this generation by finding a distraction, but I couldn't because I never properly mourned your absence. It's now that I have no distractions, just trying to find peace that I'm struggling to move on. It's like I need some sort of closure from you and I'm slowly trying to accept the fact that I'm not going to get it. I'm trying to let Leonardo go but it's so hard.

I know everyone is going to have some sort of story that they're going to tell their daughter one day, when they come to their mother and say that they got their heart broken. Like for example " Oh when I was your age I thought I was going to marry this boy named Leonardo, and then I met your father" But I was hoping and praying that this is not how this story would end, I was hoping that I would get to tell her, "I met your father when I was 15 and he was 16, he left for a while, but he came back and never left my side, and then we had you."

But unfortunately, I am going to have to tell my daughter this story and maybe even show her these very pages. But you want to know what's the difference between me and you Leo?

You would never mention this story to your daughter if she came to you heartbroken. Because if you did, you would be just as guilty as the guy who just broke your poor daughter's heart. But one day If, and when you do have a son. What are you going to do when he comes to you and says, "I just lead this girl on, I feel so bad she thought I was in love with her and everything? Do you have any advice Dad? What should I do?" Or when your sister comes to you crying, and tells you that some guy stood her up. I guarantee your mind is going to take you back to this very moment. You're going to remember me. You will remember what you did to somebody else's daughter, and somebody else's sister.

But like I've mentioned multiple times I don't hate you, but what I have mentioned is that I am extremely disappointed. I believe somewhere in that heart of yours, if you were going to end it after seeing me, you had good intentions. But you executed it horribly.

Because I couldn't understand that someone I admired, and thought was so perfect, didn't allow us to have a perfect ending.

[CHAPTER 5

a c c e p t a n c e & d i s a p o i n t m e n t]

It's only taken me until now that as I write I realise, none of this had anything to do with me, or my looks, or my personality. I no longer need to blame myself. I no longer need to feel like you left because of me. I realised that I was different to the other girls Leo typically went for. You may be asking yourself, how was she different? What made her different from any other girl? Well, Leo seemed to like easy girls, girls he could use with no attachment just simply pleasure, if you understand what I'm getting at. But he knew, I wasn't like those girls. But Leo, what you don't realise is that these easy girls don't care about you, relatively close to how I cared about you. There's one realisation you're going to come to. Which I truly do wish that you come to it very soon. It's that these so called "easy girls" are not going to make very good mothers of your children. You may be willing to deny a lot of things but I sure as hell know you wouldn't want your daughter sneaking out at late hours, risking her life, just to hook up with some guy that probably barely has any interest in her but she's afraid to lose him, so she does what he says. Or you wouldn't want you sister lying to your parents to go sleep with some guy in a park because she's scared he won't like her anymore doesn't do as he says. But the girl, that asked how your little sister was going at school, and constantly cared for you. But wouldn't deprive herself of her morals just to keep you, she would have made an amazing mother to your children.

Now you can say a lot of things Leo, but one thing I'm proud of myself is that I realised soon enough that I wasn't just some easy girl. You can brag to your friends about how you disappeared from my life. But one thing you cannot say is that you "used" me. Because I gave you absolutely nothing to use. You didn't take anything from me, well actually I tell a lie, you took my happiness. That is the one thing you can say you took, my happiness along with you when you left. No point harping on it now.

I like to be in control of things, I like to control when I feel happy and when I feel sad. This is the one thing I can't control. I can't control the fact that Leonardo left, and I can't get him back, and there's nothing I can do about it.

Whoever seems to be laying eyes on these very pages, I want you to think to yourself, knowing everything you know about me and this story. Even though you don't know me personally. Would you give up hope? Would you move on?. I know there's only one right decision to be made for when the day comes that he realises what I mentioned earlier. I just don't know whether I should let go. I've painted 2 paintings for you about Leonardo. The first one is the beautiful version of him, the caring, loving, bold and sympathetic Leonardo. The other is a self-absorbed, careless person, who doesn't care about the feelings of the people around him when making decisions. Now I don't know how to make the choice whether to hold on to the beautiful version and let go of the self-absorbed. Or to keep remembering the self-absorbed and forget the beautiful side of him since it didn't last long enough before I saw his true colours.

Lightning Source UK Ltd.
Milton Keynes UK
UKHW022037010822
406702UK00008B/269/J